this book belongs to

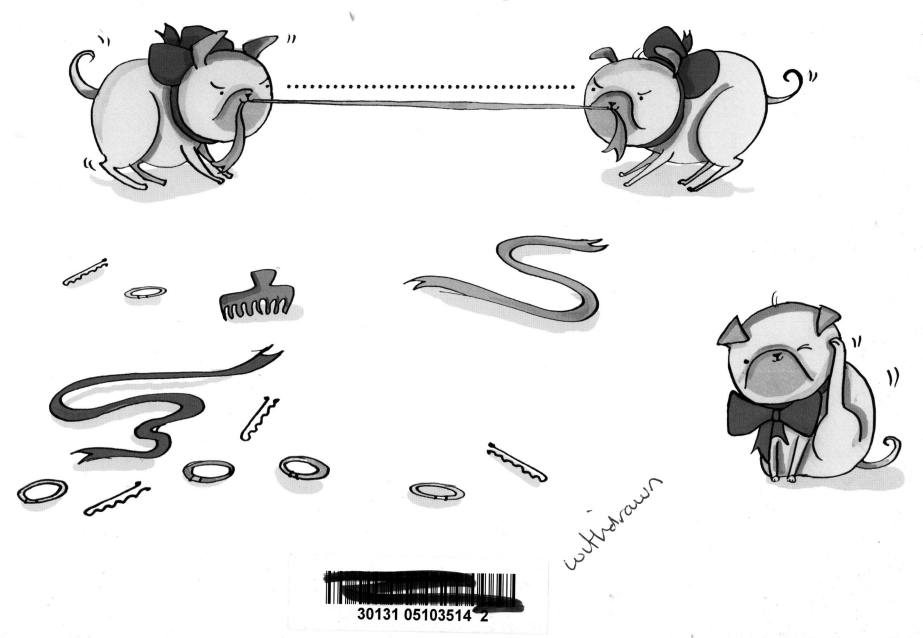

THE FAIRYTALE HAIRDRESSER AND CINDERELLA
A RED FOX BOOK 978 0 552 56535 6

Published in Great Britain by Red Fox,
an imprint of Random House Children's Publishers UK
A Random House Group Company
This edition published 2012

1 3 5 7 9 10 8 6 4 2

Text copyright © Abie Longstaff, 2012
Illustrations copyright © Lauren Beard, 2012
The right of Abie Longstaff and Lauren Beard to be identified as the author and illustrator of
this work has been asserted in accordance with the Copyright, Designs and Patents Act 1988.

Red Fox Books are published by Random House Children's Publishers UK,
61–63 Uxbridge Road, London W5 5SA

www.randomhousechildrens.co.uk
www.randomhouse.co.uk

Addresses for companies within The Random
House Group Limited can be found at:
www.randomhouse.co.uk/offices.htm THE
RANDOM HOUSE GROUP
Limited Reg. No. 954009

A CIP catalogue record for this book is
available from the British Library.
Printed in China

FSC
www.fsc.org
MIX
Paper from
responsible sources
FSC® C009967

The Random House Group Limited supports the Forest Stewardship Council (FSC®), the leading international
forest certification organization. Our books carrying the FSC label are printed on FSC®certified paper.
FSC is the only forest certification scheme endorsed by the leading environmental organizations, including
Greenpeace. Our paper procurement policy can be found at www.randomhouse.co.uk/environment.

Love, Jas ♡

You're the best, Little M×

My hair's so soft and comfy now, Princess P×

Thanks K,

for my hair

AND my prince! ×

For Grandma - L.B.
For K&E and for Harry, Lottie and Bump - A.L.

The Fairytale Hairdresser and Cinderella

Abie Longstaff & Lauren Beard

RED FOX

Kittie Lacey was the best hairdresser in all the land.

The queues for her salon twisted down the street,
out of town and all the way up the hill.

Kittie was so busy washing and
combing and cutting and styling,
she barely had time for a cup of tea.

R♥yal Ball

Everyone in the Kingdom is invited to a *perfect* ball to find my son the *perfect* girl.

8.pm. to midnight.

Then one day there was an invitation from the Queen.

Everyone got one . . .

except one person.

"Gosh," said Kittie.
"Every maiden in the land
will want her hair done!
I'm going to be even busier now."

So Kittie decided to ask for some help . . .

and Cinderella was just the girl she needed.

She started the very next day. Cinderella was excellent at . . .

sweeping,

washing,

cleaning

and making tea. At first this was all she knew how to do.

But week-by-week Cinderella watched Kittie, and week-by-week she learned. Soon she knew how to . . .

comb beards,

shave fur,

and even wash and dye wool.

Kittie was so pleased with Cinderella's
work, she gave her a beautiful glass hairclip.
"Thank you!" said Cinderella.
"I'll wear it every day!"

On the day of the Royal Ball, Kittie and Cinderella
were called to the palace to style the Queen's hair.

The Queen wanted something
Perfect
and it took Kittie and Cinderella
nearly the whole afternoon.

"Quick," said Kittie, as soon as they had finished.
"We'd better hurry back to the salon."
They rushed down the corridor,
round the corner and . . .

crash! straight into Prince Charming.

"Oh no! I'm so sorry!" said Cinderella, blushing.
"Here, this fell from your hair," said the Prince,
looking right into Cinderella's eyes as he
handed her the sparkling glass hair clip.
"I hope I see you at the ball tonight."
"Er, yes!" said Cinderella.
"Perfect!" said the Prince.

"Oh, Kittie!" said Cinderella sadly. "I can't go to the ball. I didn't get an invitation. Everyone was supposed to get one, but I don't know where mine went."

"You can come to the ball with me." said Kittie, giving Cinderella a hug. "The Queen needs us to be on hand for her hair."

"But I've nothing to wear," said poor Cinderella. "I can't go in this!"
"Don't worry, love," said Kittie.
"I know what to do."

Kittie opened her overflowing wardrobe . . . "I've been given a few bits and pieces over the years," she said.

At last they found a dress that was perfect for Cinderella. Then Kittie washed and brushed Cinderella's hair until it shone.

"There you go," she said. "You look lovely!"
"Oh, thank you, Kittie!" said Cinderella.

The Palace ballroom was filled with guests from all over the land.
Prince Charming looked for the beautiful girl he had met earlier.
But she was nowhere to be seen . . .

Upstairs Kittie and Cinderella were pinning the Queen's perfect curls.

Downstairs every maiden wanted to dance with the Prince . . .

Later, the Prince went upstairs to search for his girl. But he couldn't see her anywhere.

Meanwhile, Kittie and Cinderella had come downstairs and were dancing their best party moves. Cinderella looked for the Prince – where was he?

It felt like no time at all before –
BONG! BONG! BONG! – the clock
chimed midnight. The ball was over.
It was time to go home.

"Oh no!" said the Prince. "Where is she?"
Suddenly, on the other side of the
room, a sparkle caught his eye.

"There you are," cried the Prince. "My perfect girl!"
"Me?" said Cinderella, "I'm not perfect. This isn't even my dress."
"Well, you're perfect for me," said the Prince.

Everyone gasped as he swept her into
his arms for the last dance.

(And later, for a perfect kiss . . .)

Cinderella and the Prince were married the very next week.
The Queen was delighted that they were such a perfect match.

Kittie was pleased to see
Cinderella so happy.

But would Cinderella ever have time to come to the salon again?

Of course she would!
Nowadays Cinderella
and her prince help out
as often as they can.

And whenever there's a Royal Ball, Kittie is always ready with a fairytale hairstyle for her best friend, Princess Cinderella.